Hippo Books
Scholastic Publications Limited
London

This book is part of the J M Barrie 'Peter Pan Bequest'.
This means that Sir J M Barrie's royalty on this book goes to help cure the children who are lying ill in the Great Ormond Street Hospital for Sick Children, London.

The full text of *Peter Pan* is available in hardback from Hodder and Stoughton Limited.

Scholastic Publications Ltd.,
10 Earlham Street, London WC2H 9LN, UK

Scholastic Inc.,
730 Broadway, New York, NY 10003, USA

Scholastic Tab Publications Ltd.,
123 Newkirk Road, Richmond Hill,
Ontario L4C 3G5, Canada

Ashton Scholastic Pty. Ltd.,
PO Box 579, Gosford, New South Wales,
Australia

Ashton Scholastic Ltd.,
165 Marua Road, Panmure, Auckland 6,
New Zealand

This edition first published by Scholastic Publications Limited, 1985

Reprinted 1988
ISBN 0 590 70281 5

Made and printed in Spain by Mateu Cromo, Madrid
Typeset in Plantin by Keyline Graphics, London NW6

The Darlings lived in a quiet street in Chelsea. There were Mr and Mrs Darling and their three children – Wendy, John and Little Michael. They were an ordinary family except for one thing – they employed a big Newfoundland dog – called Nana – as nursemaid to the children.

Every evening, Mrs Darling told the children bedtime stories of princes and princesses, pirates and little lost boys, and sat with them until they went to sleep.

One evening as Mrs Darling sat by the fire sewing, a strange boy appeared at the window. Nana was wide awake, leapt at the boy and caught his shadow. Mrs Darling rolled it up neatly, put it in a drawer, and forgot about it. But Peter Pan did not forget his shadow.

One evening when Mr and Mrs Darling were going out, they came into the nursery to say goodnight. Nana was tidying up. Mr Darling tripped over her and lost his temper.

"The children are too old for a nursemaid, and Wendy should have a room of her own," he roared. "Tonight is her last night in the nursery."

He dragged Nana into the garden and tied her to a tree. Mr and Mrs Darling went out, leaving the children asleep and Nana on guard in the garden.

Suddenly a boy appeared on the nursery window sill! It was Peter Pan. He had come back with his fairy friend, Tinker Bell, to find his shadow. He found it in the drawer, and accidentally shut Tinker Bell inside! She was furious. Wendy

woke up and saw him trying to stick his shadow on with soap.
"I'll sew it back on for you," she said. As she sewed, Peter Pan told her all about Never-Never Land and the Lost Boys.

He said he loved listening to their bedtime stories and used to fly back and tell them to the others.

"Tell me how the story of the girl with the glass slipper ends," he pleaded. And Wendy told him the story of Cinderella.

"Come back with me and tell stories to the Lost Boys, Wendy," he said.

Wendy thought that was a wonderful idea, as long as Michael and John could go too.

"But we can't fly," she said.

"I'll teach you," cried Peter. "Just think lovely thoughts and they lift you into the air."

He suddenly remembered Tinker Bell stuck in the drawer and hurried to let her out while Wendy woke John and Michael. Peter then sprinkled them with some fairy dust and suddenly they were flying. Round and round the room they zoomed, then out of the window they flew, while Nana barked frantically in the garden below.

"Second star on the right and straight on till morning," said Peter.

"There's Never-Never Land," Peter pointed. "Look there's the Indian Camp – the Indians are our friends – and there's the pirate ship. It is captained by the worst pirate in the world, Captain Hook."

"Is he big?" whispered John.

"Not as big as he was," said Peter.

He told them how once, long ago, he had fought the Captain and cut off one of his hands. Ever since the Captain had worn a hook. Peter had thrown the hand to a crocodile, which had followed the Captain ever since hoping for the rest of him! Some time in the past the crocodile had also swallowed a clock, so the Captain always knew from the "tick tock" when he was close.

Down on the pirate ship Hook was wondering how to get his

own back on Peter Pan. Suddenly, there came a call from the Crow's Nest, "Peter Pan ahoy!"

"Where?" shouted Hook. Then he saw Peter Pan, with Wendy, John and Michael flying above them.

"Pipe up the crew," yelled Hook. "We've got him this time. Fire!" Cannonballs flew towards the children.

"Look out," called Peter. "Tink, take Wendy and the boys to the house. I'll draw their fire."

Tinker Bell was very jealous of Wendy as Peter seemed to like her so much. She rather hoped that the children would not be able to keep up with her and be lost, and she sped on ahead.

She flew swiftly through the jungle down into a clearing beside the Hangman's Tree. As she landed a secret door flew open in the hollow tree and down the tunnel Tinker Bell flew. She landed at the bottom in the hidden house of Peter Pan.

"Ting-a-Ling," she tinkled, flying around the room trying to wake up the Lost Boys.

"Hallo Tink," said a voice. "Where have you been? What is

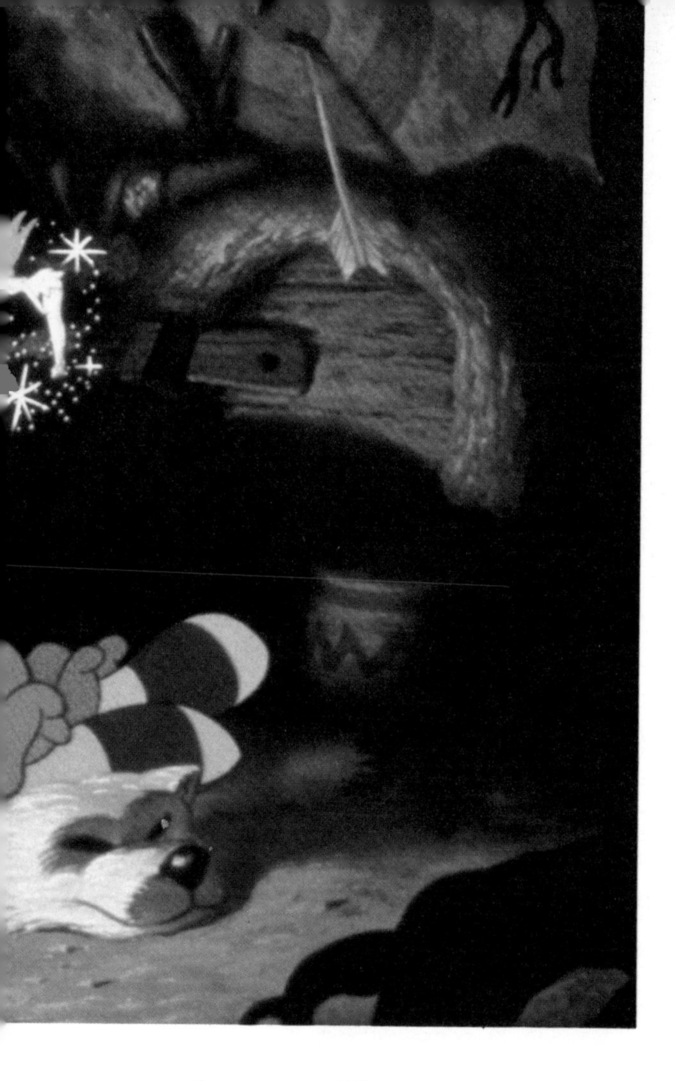

the matter?"

"Peter wants you to shoot the Wendy bird. Quick, quick, Peter will be so pleased."

One of the boys hastily fitted an arrow to his bow, and when Wendy, John and Michael appeared, the Lost Boys pelted them with sticks and stones, especially Wendy. Down she dropped. Peter swooped to her rescue. "I brought her to be a mother to us all and tell us stories," he said. "We must look after her."

Wendy, John and Michael soon settled in, and Peter Pan wanted to show off his island.

"Come on, Wendy," he cried. "There is so much to see. I'll show you the mermaids and the boys will take John and Michael to hunt some Indians!"

The boys marched off through the forest. There were wild animals all around them, but no one was frightened.

"Let's surround the Indians and take them by surprise," suggested John. But it was the boys who were surprised. The

Indians had disguised themselves as trees, and soon had the boys surrounded.

They bound the boys with ropes and marched them off to their village.

The Lost Boys tried to comfort Michael and John. "Don't worry," they said. "The Indians are our friends." Michael and John were not so sure. The Chief looked anything but friendly.

Wendy and Peter had flown off to the mermaid lagoon on the far side of the island. As they sat talking to the mermaids, Peter suddenly said "Hush!" A boat from the pirate ship was going by with Captain Hook and his faithful cook, Smee, on board. In the stern sat Tiger Lily, the daughter of the Indian Chief, tied up with ropes.

"You will tell us where Peter Pan lives," said the Captain. "Otherwise, I will leave you tied to Skull Rock while the tide comes in and you will drown." But brave Tiger Lily refused to say a word.

Peter and Wendy flew to Skull Rock and waited for Captain Hook. He tied the Princess to the rock as the water began to rise. Peter leapt from behind the rock, his knife at the ready. The Captain, red with rage, pulled his sword. All over the cave they fought until Peter beat the Captain and freed Tiger Lily.

Off they flew to the Indian Camp; the Chief was so delighted to have his daughter back he immediately freed all the captives and invited them to a wonderful feast. During the dancing he made Peter Pan an Indian Chief, and promised that his braves would always guard the home of Peter Pan and the Lost Boys.

While they were all celebrating at the Indian Camp, the faithful Smee managed to capture Tinker Bell. He proudly took her to Captain Hook.

"Why Miss Bell," said the Captain sweetly. "I have heard that Peter Pan treats you very badly now Wendy has arrived. If we knew where Peter Pan lived, we could kidnap Wendy and make her work for us. You would no longer be bothered with her."

"You won't hurt Peter?" Tink asked in a quiet tinkle.

"Of course not," said the crafty Captain.

And Tink believed him.

She flew across to the map of Never-Never Land and pointed to the place where Peter and the Lost Boys lived.

Despite all their adventures, Wendy and John and Michael were beginning to feel that they would like to go home. That evening Wendy talked to the Lost Boys about their home, about Mr and Mrs Darling, and Nana, and the stories they read and the places they went. All the boys began to feel very homesick.

"Come back with us," said Wendy. "Oh, yes," they cried. "Let's go now!"

"I will never leave," said Peter Pan. "I will stay here forever."

Wendy and the boys sorrowfully said goodbye to him and climbed up the tunnel.

But there at the entrance in the woods waited Hook and his pirate crew. They had overcome the Indian braves and as each boy emerged from the tunnel, he was captured and tied up with ropes.

The last person to come out was Wendy – there was no Peter! A disgusted Captain Hook gathered together his men and their captives and ordered them back to the ship. But before he left the clearing, he and Smee put a bomb wrapped in paper like a present and addressed "To Peter From Wendy" at the hidden door.

They hoped that when Peter Pan came out, he would rip open the parcel and blow himself out of Never-Never Land for ever.

Back on board the ship, Tink was horrified when she saw the pirates arrive with the captives. It was all her fault. What could she do? At least they had not captured Peter. The pirates were far too busy with their prisoners to notice Tink slip away and fly off to warn Peter Pan.

The boys were given the choice to join the pirate crew or walk the plank. They all immediately decided it would be great fun to be pirates! Only Wendy refused.

"Very well, my dear," said Captain Hook. "You will have the honour of being the one to walk the plank."

A blindfold was tied round Wendy's eyes and rough hands guided her to the plank. She walked bravely along it and then disappeared. Everyone on deck waited anxiously for a splash, but none came. Instead they heard the familiar happy crow of Peter Pan. He had arrived just in time to scoop up Wendy in mid-air and fly her to safety.

"You have gone too far this time, Captain," taunted Peter. He drew his sword and swooped down from the rigging.

What a fight it was. First Captain Hook had the advantage then Peter. While they battled Tink, who thought she ought to do something to make up for betraying Peter, cut the ropes that bound the boys. They immediately turned on the pirates and forced them to abandon ship in a rowing boat. Then Peter cleverly knocked Hook's sword from his hand. Hook knew he was finished and leapt overboard, swimming desperately after

the fast disappearing rowing boat. And close behind Captain Hook followed the crocodile – "Tick ... tock ... tick ... tock..."

Peter immediately took command of the ship. "Set the sails," he called. "We're leaving for London."

"Oh John, oh Michael," cried Wendy. "We're going home!"

As she spoke the pirate ship rose gently from the sea and sailed off through the clouds.

Poor Mr and Mrs Darling had given up hope of ever seeing their children again. Every night Mrs Darling sat by the fire in the nursery with the window open just in case the children returned. She was fast asleep and did not see the ship as it hovered outside the window.

"Let's slip into our beds as if we had never been away," said Wendy.

Mr and Mrs Darling could not believe their beloved children had returned. They watched with Wendy as the shadow of a ship, sailed by a boy who would never grow up, passed silently across the face of the moon, returning to Never-Never Land.